The Unexplained

THE SUPERNATURAL

By
Rhiannon Lassiter

GARETH**STEVENS**
PUBLISHING
A Member of the WRC Media Family of Companies

Please visit our web site at: www.garethstevens.com
For a free color catalog describing Gareth Stevens Publishing's
list of high-quality books and multimedia programs,
call 1-800-542-2595 or 1-800-387-3178 (Canada).
Gareth Stevens Publishing's fax: (414) 332-3567.

Library of Congress Cataloging-in-Publication Data

Lassiter, Rhiannon.
    The Supernatural / Rhiannon Lassiter. — North American ed.
      p. cm. — (The unexplained)
    Includes bibliographical references and index.
    ISBN 0-8368-6267-8 (lib. bdg.)
    1. Parapsychology—Juvenile literature. 2. Occultism—Juvenile literature.
    I. Title. II. Series.
    BF1031.L29   2006
    130—dc22   2005054079

This North American edition first published in 2006 by
Gareth Stevens Publishing
A Member of the WRC Media Family of Companies
330 West Olive Street, Suite 100
Milwaukee, WI 53212 USA

This U.S. edition copyright © 2006 by Gareth Stevens, Inc. Original
edition copyright © 2003 by ticktock Entertainment Ltd. First published
in Great Britain in 2003 by ticktock Publishing Ltd., Unit 2, Orchard
Business Centre, North Farm Road, Tunbridge Wells, Kent, TN2 3XF.

Gareth Stevens editor: Monica Rausch
Gareth Stevens art direction: Tammy West

Picture Credits: t = top, b = bottom, c = center, l = left, r= right,
OFC = outside front cover, OBC = outside back cover, IFC = inside
front cover
AKG; 5br, 4tl, 8/9b, 12cb, 14tl, 18c, 23c, 26tl, 33cr. Ann Ronan @ Image
Select; 4bl, 6/7t, 10tl, 17c, 19tr. British Museum; 15t. Colorific; 14/15c.
Corbis; 6/7b, 10bl, 14/15b & OBC, 20bl, 28cl, 28tl, 28/29c. e.t.archive;
8/9t. Fortean; 4c, 7tr, 8c, 8/9c, 10/11b, 12l, 12/13c, 13bl, 16 (main pic),
16/17t, 17b, 17tr, 18b, 24bl, 24/25b, 28b, 29b, 28/29t, 30cb, 30/31c,
31br, 31tr, 32tl. Gamma; IFC, 9t. Geoscience; 6bl. Image Select; 11br,
18/19b, 20c, 27tr, 33t. Images; 20tl. Science Photo Library; 26bl, 26/27c.
Telegraph Colour Library; OFC (main pic), 10c. Tony Stone; 14bl, 21tr,
20/21c, 22, 24c, 24tl, 27c, 32/33 (main).Werner Foreman; 5tr.

Printed in the United States of America

1 2 3 4 5 6 7 8 10 9 09 08 07 06

CONTENTS

THE FUTURE REVEALED

In many ancient civilizations, the ability to predict the future was not considered a magical power but rather a useful ability. Today, people tend to be more skeptical about this so-called "psychic" power. Among believers, however , many methods are used to tell the future, from crystal balls to tarot cards, astrology to palm reading.

WITCHES AND WARLOCKS

n the past, when certain events were beyond human understanding, people tended to believe these events were caused by a supernatural being or by a human with supernatural powers. Through the centuries, scholars and scientists have sought explanations for a variety of so-called psychic phenomena, but many mysterious occurrences remain unexplained. Before we can examine the evidence and unravel the mysteries, we must first explore past beliefs in the paranormal.

What do YOU think ?

The author Arthur C. Clarke wrote, "Any sufficiently advanced technology is indistinguishable from magic." Many of the advanced technologies we have today—radios, computers, and airplanes—would have appeared "magical" to our ancestors. As humans, we often seek explanations for what we do not understand, and magic can be used to explain almost any phenomenon. It may be that some undiscovered technologies or yet-unknown scientific forces could explain some of today's mysterious phenomena.

THE COURT MAGICIAN

Dr. John Dee (1527-1608), an English mathematician and astrologer (right), studied sorcery and practiced magic for several European royal courts. He claimed angels had taught him magic spells as well as the language Enoch, which Adam supposedly spoke in the biblical Garden of Eden. His influence proved to be great. Queen Elizabeth I chose January 14 for her coronation because Dr. Dee told her the date was astrologically fortunate. A black crystal, which he said an angel had given him, is now on display at the British Museum.

MAGIC OF THE GODS

Hieroglyphics and magical inscriptions adorned the temples of the Egyptian goddess Isis, the goddess of love, death, cunning, and magic. Ancient gods and goddesses such as Isis (opposite) were believed to hold mysteries that only their followers were allowed to learn. Their followers worshiped them by performing magic rituals. Becoming one with the god or goddess—or at least obtaining his or her supernatural powers—was often a follower's goal. Because *Isis* means "wisdom," her initiates were expected to be intelligent. Plutarch, an ancient Greek philosopher, described Isis worshipers as seekers of the hidden truths behind the gods.

DEADLY NIGHTSHADE

Belladonna, or deadly nightshade (below), is an extremely poisonous herb that was said to be used in magic rituals and potions. When eaten in very small doses, the herb can cause people to hallucinate and feel like they are flying. This feeling may be why some people started to associate witches with flying.

BLACK HATS AND BROOMSTICKS

Women believed to have magic powers often were called witches. According to folklore about them, witches past and present wear black (right), ride a broomstick, brew magic potions in a cauldron, and have a spirit helper, or familiar, often in the form of a cat. If any of these characteristics were true, witches would be very easy to spot. In the past, many women in Europe and the United States were persecuted for being witches just because they lived alone, used herbs to cure illnesses, or disagreed with certain religious teachings.

A DEMONIC DEAL

Many Christians once believed warlocks, or men who supposedly had magical powers, and witches were in league with the devil. People believed the devil gave them magical powers in return for their souls. Anyone who claimed he or she could do magic was therefore believed to be "unholy." The English dramatist Christopher Marlowe (1564-93) and the German poet Johann Wolfgang von Goethe (1749-1832) both wrote plays about Johann Faust (1480-1538), a legendary German magician who sold his soul to the devil in return for great wisdom. Faust is shown here (right) standing within the protection of a ritual circle . He has summoned Mephistopheles, an agent of the devil.

Many customs and superstitions are based on a belief in magic. Some customs are designed to ward off evil influences, and they attribute magic powers to certain items. A horseshoe hung over a doorway, for example, is thought to prevent witches from entering.

BLACK AND WHITE MAGIC

ccording to some beliefs about magic, magic practices can be separated into two categories: black magic and white magic. Black magic includes rituals that make use of blood, death, or the name of the devil. White magic involves powers of healing, visions, and prayer. Today, not all of the people who practice magic think of themselves as either black or white magicians. Some of these people believe magic is a type of science that can be used for good *or* evil. Others deliberately choose to study either only white or only black magic.

What do YOU think ?

People once found witchcraft convenient to blame for many misfortunes. If a cow fell sick or a crop was diseased, it may have been easier to blame a weak old woman and her supposed "witchcraft" than to accept the events as results of mismanagement or simply bad luck. Sometimes the fear of witches created hysteria throughout an entire community. People often would join in accusing a person of being a witch out of fear of being accused of witchcraft themselves. In 1692 in Salem, Massachusetts, for example, more than 150 people were arrested in anti-witchcraft hysteria. In seventeenth-century Europe, even a birthmark could brand a person as a witch. During witch-hunting hysteria there, over 40,000 people were executed in Great Britain alone.

CRYSTAL HEALING

Crystals (left) and semi-precious stones have long been said to have magical healing powers. In Egypt, magicians sometimes advised people to eat the powdered remains of magical amulets to cure illness. Today, crystal healers continue to claim they can cure minor illnesses with crystals. To make use of a crystal's healing powers, it is often simply placed against the skin of a patient. Sometimes, however, it is still ground into a powder and eaten.

DEVIL WORSHIP

Black magicians who made pacts, or deals, with the devil reportedly held ceremonies to worship him. A Black Mass, for example, was a corruption of a Christian's worship service and was designed to summon the devil. It was said to involve acts of deliberate evil in order to please the devil. Another ceremony, the Witches' Sabbat (below), was supposedly a midnight ritual in which witches and demons danced around a fire. The ceremony probably is connected to older Celtic festivals held on May Day and Halloween. Although practicing witches today do hold a Witches' Sabbat, the ceremony is not necessarily connected with the intent to summon the devil. It can be held as a celebration of birth and new life.

SOLOMON THE MAGICIAN

Solomon, one of the biblical kings of Israel, was said to be a great magician. The *Key of Solomon*, one of the oldest known books of spells, tells how he supposedly "discovered the secret of how to shut a million satanic spirits in a bottle of black glass, together with seventy-two of their kings." The book was used by black magicians because it also supposedly told how to make a pact with the devil, summon spirits, gain fortunes, and extend life. Solomon's Seal (above), two interlocked triangles, often is used in magic rites. Solomon's Seal resembles the Star of David, a symbol of Judaism named after Solomon's father, King David.

VOODOO

Voodoo is a religion practiced mainly in parts of Africa, South America, and the Caribbean. It includes a combination of Catholic and West African beliefs and traditions (left). Like many other religions, voodoo has a dark side. Some voodoo sorcerers claim they can create zombies— people who are raised from the dead and obey a sorcerer's commands. Some sorcerers also make voodoo dolls of a living person, using that person's hair or nail clippings. Sticking pins into the doll is believed to harm the person it represents.

What do YOU think ?

Strong faith perhaps can allow people to perform actions that they are normally not capable of accomplishing. Studies of fakirs, for example, have shown that, with training and faith, the human mind and body are capable of extraordinary feats. Research suggests that fakirs can use a mixture of self-hypnosis and exceptional muscle control to perform their feats. It could mean that we are all capable of performing these amazing acts, but fakirs have the advantage of great self-belief and self-control.

MIRACULOUS POWERS

Many people believe in the existence of miraculous events and powers, especially when religious leaders or prophets are said to have them. Religious believers sometimes claim their God or gods bestow powers on certain people in times of crisis. Almost every major religion has accounts of miracles performed by priests or saints who possessed unusual and powerful abilities. The existence of these powers is difficult to prove scientifically—but equally difficult to disprove. How strong is the human power of belief, and how might it play a role in these miracles?

STIGMATA

Stigmata are physical wounds resembling the five wounds left on Jesus Christ after he was nailed to the cross. Since Jesus' crucifixion, stigmata have appeared spontaneously on certain people, such as Antonio Ruffini (below). Usually, the people who experience stigmata are fervent Christians, but they often have nothing else in common. Stigmata do not seem to be caused by disease or self-inflicted injury. Some people's wounds last for years, while others' wounds heal quickly. Today, stigmata remain a scientific mystery. Some cases are considered by the Roman Catholic Church to be miracles.

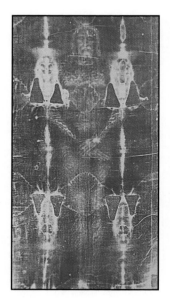

THE TURIN SHROUD

The Turin Shroud (left), first displayed in 1353, has the image of a crucified man imprinted on it. It was said to be the burial sheet of Jesus Christ. In 1989, scientific carbon-dating tests were used to determine the shroud's age. The test results placed the date of the shroud's origin between A.D. 1260 and 1390—centuries after Christ's burial. Some people, however, have claimed anti-clerical scientists faked the results. Today, the shroud still is honored as a holy relic.

HEALING POWERS

Certain religious statues, such as the Madonna at Lourdes in France (left), are believed to have miraculous healing powers. Every year, thousands of people make pilgrimages to these statues to receive cures for illnesses ranging from minor to deadly. For many of the travelers, the journey is their last hope of becoming well. They often experience some immediate beneficial effects from the visit, but it has yet to be proven that visitors experience long-term health improvements.

THE RESURRECTION OF CHRIST

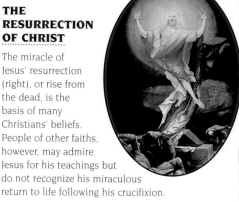

The miracle of Jesus' resurrection (right), or rise from the dead, is the basis of many Christians' beliefs. People of other faiths, however, may admire Jesus for his teachings but do not recognize his miraculous return to life following his crucifixion.

FAKIRS

Fakirs are religious men in India and Pakistan who are said to enter a trancelike state and perform astounding feats of endurance. In 1835, the Maharaja of Lahore asked a fakir named Haridas to demonstrate his abilities. Haridas was buried underground in a locked coffin, and barley was sown in the earth above it. Forty days later, Haridas was dug up and found alive and well. Fakirs still give displays of their powers, which include lying unhurt on a bed of nails (below), walking on hot coals, and levitating.

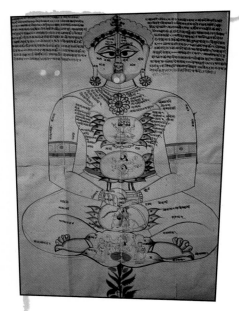

MAGIC ENERGIES, PSYCHIC POWERS

Different belief systems have different ways of treating so-called psychic powers and energies. In some belief systems, psychic phenomena are part of the religious activities. People subscribing to these systems believe supernatural powers and energies are part of normal life. They often try to live according to complex rituals surrounding these powers and energies. Others subscribe to belief systems in which any manifestation of the supernatural is feared. They try to ignore any evidence of or reference to the supernatural.

CHAKRA POINTS

Chakra is the Hindu word for a main center of spiritual power believed to be on the human body. According to some Hindu beliefs, seven main chakras exist on the body. Raw energy is said to be drawn from Earth through the chakra points, where it is transformed into a usable form. Detailed maps of chakras and their connecting pathways have been used in Eastern belief systems and health care for thousands of years (above).

LEGENDARY TREASURES

Some traditional pagan beliefs involved legendary items of great power. In mythology, these treasures are usually a sword, a spear, a cup (right), and a stone. Each item has different powers and stories attached to it. Legends, for example, tell of the Cauldron of Dagda, a cup of plenty said to provide a never-ending supply of food. Magical objects are also used as symbols in the Tarot, a deck of cards used in fortune-telling. During World War II, German leader Adolf Hitler collected some of these legendary magical objects, believing they would make him invincible.

RITUAL PAINTINGS

The life of the Navaho Indians, Native Americans who live in Arizona and New Mexico, involves close attention to rituals and magical rites. The Navaho live in harmony with the environment and carry out their daily activities with customs and chants intended to bring good fortune and ward off evil. One of their most impressive rituals is the curing ceremony, presided over by a medicine man, or spiritual leader. The ceremony involves drawing elaborate paintings in sand (left), which the Navaho believe help cure illness.

CHI ENERGY

Healing through acupuncture involves a belief in *chi*, a vital energy that is said to exist in all things. In acupuncture, pain and illness are believed to be caused by an imbalance or an improper flow of chi through the body. Needles are inserted along the pathways chi is believed to travel to help reroute or balance the chi. Chi often is believed to consist of two opposite, complementary forces, *yin* and *yang*. Yin is feminine and negatively charged; yang is masculine and positively charged. Each contains part of the other, as seen in the yin-yang symbol at the center of this image (left). It is said that a master of *chi* can infuse an object with more *chi*. The Sony Corporation funded a seven-year project into this psychic phenomenon. In tests, a *chi* practitioner attempted to project *chi* energy into one of two glasses of water. A second *chi* practitioner then attempted to identify the glass that had more *chi* energy. The tests were said to have had a 70 percent success rate, although some people have doubted their validity.

What do YOU think ?

Well-established belief systems, such as a belief in *chi*, can be as clearly thought out and as consistent as conventional scientific knowledge. In China, for example, acupuncture, a treatment based on the chi system, has been accepted as scientifically valid for hundreds of years. Western doctors, however, were slow to take it seriously as a medical treatment. Other healing systems could offer similar benefits if doctors considered and studied them.

BLOOD MAGIC

Many spiritual beliefs involve a belief in a certain power found in blood or surrounding blood. Voodoo and African shamanism, for example, include rituals that involve sacrificing animals, often roosters or goats (right), and performing certain ceremonies with the blood. Even the Bible contains many references to the sacrifice of animals as a way of paying tribute to God.

TRICKSTER OR PSYCHIC?

Grigori Rasputin (c.1871-1916) (left) was a Siberian monk whose activities damaged the credibility of all psychic research in Russia for many years. He was politically ambitious, and he gained considerable power at the court of Nicholas II, the last czar of Russia (1894-1917). Rasputin claimed his "supernatural powers" could cure Alexei, the czar's only son, of hemophilia. He was able to convince the czarina of his abilities, but the royal family's strong belief in Rasputin damaged their own reputation. Rasputin was eventually assassinated by Russian nobles jealous of his great influence.

GRAND MASTER OF THE GOLDEN DAWN

Aleister Crowley (1875-1947) (right) wanted to be known as "the wickedest man alive." He became grand master of a secret society called the Golden Dawn, but he was expelled for extreme practices. Eventually, he came to believe he was a vampire and used a variety of drugs to enhance his "magical" powers. He attracted many followers during and after his lifetime. He once said, "I may be a black magician, but I'm a bloody great one."

SIMPLY TRICKS

Harry Houdini (above) was an escapologist and magician who faked psychic abilities on stage. Because Houdini knew how to fake psychic powers, he did not believe they actually existed. He published a book titled A Magician Among the Spirits in an attempt to discredit mediums and others who claimed to have psychic powers.

PSYCHICS OR MAGICIANS?

Magic shows and other stage shows offer displays of supposedly paranormal phenomena and psychic powers as entertainment. Some stage magicians freely admit that their feats, such as mind-reading and levitation, are simply tricks, while others claim to have genuine psychic abilities. Some people, such as Aleister Crowley and Grigori Rasputin, have displayed their so-called psychic powers for other motives than entertainment. They hope to gain money or power from their activities. Because Crowley and Rasputin were motivated by greed, people have doubted the authenticity of their psychic abilities.

When Scholars Know Sin • Jr. Skeptic • Psychotherapy Snake Oil

SKEPTIC

Extraordinary Claims, Revolutionary Ideas & The Promotion of Science

Vol. 5 No. 3, 1998 $5.95 USA ($7.95 Can.(Int'l))

NORM LEVITT On WHY PROFESSORS BELIEVE WEIRD THINGS

SPECIAL SECTION: • Norm Levitt On Sex, Race, & the Trials of the New Left • When Scholars Know Sin— Alternative Religions and Their Academic Supporters • Psychotherapy—The Snake Oil Of The 90s? • Memes—What Are They Good For? • Facilitated Communication: Eight Years and Counting • ALSO: • An Interview With Skeptical Parapsychologist Susan Blackmore • Four Days On Planet Randi • Waco Debate • Is God Dead?—Why Nietzsche and Time Magazine Were Wrong By Michael Shermer • The True Believers By James Randi • The Case for Yoga • The Graduate Record Exam Reexamined • Dumeth News • JR. SKEPTIC: • Bigfoot! • Crystals—Exploring the Real Magic • Testing A Dowsing Rod

PROFESSIONAL SKEPTICS

A skeptic always questions accepted beliefs and mistrusts new theories and ideas until they are scientifically proven. Even after finding scientific proof, a skeptic tends to think nothing is certain. *Skeptic* magazine (above) attempts to refute beliefs that are, in its opinion, "180 degrees out of phase with reason."

THE POWER OF THE MIND

Uri Geller (left) is a stage magician who claims to use the power of his mind to bend metal objects, restart watches, and force computers to malfunction. He has performed these feats and others under strict test conditions, but he has also been accused of being a fake. His accusers claim to have seen him falsifying his demonstrations. Since Uri Geller was originally an amateur magician, people tend to doubt his psychic abilities. The phenomenon of metal-bending is not unique to Geller. Other people claim to possess a similar power, and metallurgists, or experts in metals and their properties, also have reproduced the experiments.

What do YOU think ?

It is impossible to prove that a stage magician does not have "magical" powers. The results of a magic trick could be reproduced by non-magical means, but that does not mean the magical powers are not real. Many people, however, do not believe stage magicians have genuine magical powers. Still, people enjoy magic shows because of the skill and creativity used in the tricks. The ingenuity with which some tricks are done can be even more impressive than if magic actually is used.

SPIRITS AND SPIRITUALISM

People who claim to have psychic abilities often believe in the existence of spirits—non-physical beings thought to be gods or the souls of the dead. Some people claim they can contact spirits using their psychic powers. Among spiritualists and practitioners of magic, however, no single, consistent idea exists about what exactly "spirits" are or what methods should be used to communicate with them. Some spirits reportedly can be benevolent; they guide or teach the humans they care about. Some spirits are tricksters, and they play jokes on people who attempt to contact them. Other spirits are supposedly malicious; they are believed to return to the physical world just to cause harm.

SPIRIT GUIDES

Some shamans use spirit guides as aids and symbols in their rituals. Some Brazilian shamans believe people have spirits shaped like different animals, the most powerful of which is the jaguar. Some Native American shamans associate their powers with specific animals. A wolf shaman (above), for example, may be expected to be tireless and fierce, while a coyote shaman could be a devious trickster. Not all spirit guides are animals, however; strong images and physical symbols are also important.

What do YOU think ?

Belief in the survival of the soul or spirit after death has been widespread throughout human history. This belief may be so strong because we find it hard to believe the people we love will just stop existing when their bodies die. Some people think that if humans do have spirits, then why should other animals or objects not have spirits as well?

REINCARNATION

Many people believe that after a person dies, his or her spirit is reincarnated or reborn in another body. Some Buddhists (left) believe that good or evil deeds in one life will be rewarded or punished accordingly in the next life. In some Hindu beliefs, people who continually lead worthy lives will eventually be free of the cycle of death and rebirth and will pass on to the next stage of existence. Regression hypnotists supposedly have put people into a trancelike state in which they recall events from their previous lives. Some of the hypnotized people have even spoken in languages they do not know in their present life. It is difficult, however, to prove—or disprove—the act of reincarnation.

SPIRIT BIRDS

The ancient Egyptians believed a person has many different spiritual parts. Egyptian myths tell of great magicians who could separate their *ka*, one of their spiritual parts, from their bodies and fly in the form of birds (left). Spells played an important part in the everyday lives of the Egyptians. They believed that all words have power, and they used words to bring about desired events or to curse enemies.

DREAMTIME

Australian Aborigines have a complex set of beliefs about the supernatural powers of their ancestors. Many aboriginal beliefs involve the idea of the Dreamtime, a time before Earth and the physical world existed and when aboriginal ancestors worked to create it. As shown in rock paintings (left), Aborigines tend to see the natural world as a powerful and mysterious place with no clear distinction between the natural and the supernatural. They regard natural and supernatural events and beings as essential aspects of life.

CARETAKERS
OF BODY AND SOUL

Today, shamans throughout the world, like this one (right) from Nigeria, watch over their followers. A shaman is a spiritual leader and healer who cares for the bodies and souls of his or her people. A shaman, for example, could be asked to cure an illness or hunt for a missing soul stolen by an enemy. In many cultures, shamanism is passed on through families. Some shamans are believed to continue to serve as guardian spirits of their people even after they die.

ECTOPLASM

This medium (right) is supposedly emitting ectoplasm. Ectoplasm is reportedly a substance called up out of the medium's body to give a spirit a physical form. It is often silvery-white in color and resembles thin fabric. It forms the body and clothes of a spirit while the spirit is communicating with the medium. Touching a spirit made of ectoplasm is said to cause the medium to become ill. Although it has not been proven that all mediums fake ectoplasm, it is possible to swallow a skein of cotton and gradually regurgitate it.

REST IN PEACE?

The phrase "rest in peace" carved on tombstones implies that the dead might not necessarily "rest" or be at peace. Over the centuries, many stories have developed about ghosts who do not rest. They haunt people or places for revenge or because they have left something undone in their lives. Some people have reported that they live comfortably with supernatural neighbors. Others say ghosts are dangerous and can smash objects, make eerie noises, and create a general feeling of menace in a house.

CLAIRVOYANTS AND MEDIUMS

Clairvoyancy is one of the earliest documented psychic phenomena—and one of the most profitable for those people who claim to perform it. Clairvoyants and mediums claim they can contact the spirits of the dead. Some mediums claim only to be able to speak with a spirit, while others claim they can give a spirit some sort of physical form. Mediums have often been exposed as fakes or have admitted to being frauds. Grieving people, however, are particularly susceptible to being defrauded because they long to contact a dead loved one. Despite the many frauds, however, clairvoyancy has yet to be fully disproved.

CONTACTING THE DEAD

To contact the spirits, many mediums hold séances. In a séance, a group of people who wish to speak with a dead person form a circle around a table (right). They hold hands while the medium attempts to summon the dead person's spirit. Mediums have been known to fake the responses of spirits by using devices that strike the underside of the table, producing "ghostly" knocks in reply to questions. Some mediums, however, have produced inexplicable effects in tests designed by scientists attempting to expose them as frauds.

THE CASE OF KATIE KING

Victorian scientist William Crookes investigated the famous medium Florence Cook. Cook claimed she could manifest the spirit of Katie King (right) who appeared at séances and talked to guests. Cook, however, was suspected of dressing up as the spirit herself or of having an accomplice do so. Crookes asserted that his investigation had convinced him of the spirit's existence. Crookes did not publish his finding in any scientific journals, but he never retracted his claims. Later, it was claimed that he had supported Cook's fraud so he could have an affair with her.

QUESTIONING THE SPIRITS

In ancient times, people often asked spirits for advice. They sometimes consulted oracles, or visionaries, who went into a trance and were believed to be able to ask the spirits questions on the behalf of a person. One of the most famous oracles was Pythia, the Oracle at Delphi in Greece (above). She used volcanic fumes and medicines to assist her in her spirit visions. Although ancient and modern mediums have posed many questions to the spirits, we have yet to receive any real answers about life after death.

What do YOU think ?

If humans continue to live on as spirits after they die, then it would seem reasonable for dead spirits to want to contact living humans. Spirits of murdered people, for example, might want to identify their killers. Other spirits might hint at where they buried money when they were alive. Spirits might also want relatives to know they are happy and at peace. Fake mediums take advantage of people who are vulnerable after the death of someone they loved; the grief-stricken may pay a large fee to hear from a loved one. Mediums, however, might say they are only trying to provide comfort for the bereaved.

THE BERMUDA TRIANGLE

In 1945, five Avenger bomber planes took off from Fort Lauderdale, Florida, and disappeared without trace near the Bermudas, a small group of islands in the Atlantic Ocean. The boat sent to search for them also vanished. Since then, hundreds of other ships and planes have disappeared in that same area—a "triangle" of ocean (above) between the Bermudas, Florida, and Puerto Rico. Alien abductions, sea monsters, and unusual magnetic forces have all been offered as explanations for the disappearances.

What do YOU think

The law of probability suggests that, out of a large number of predictions, some predictions are bound to come true. Those predictions that do not come true, however, are quickly forgotten; only the "true" predictions seem to be remembered. The same law can be applied to the Bermuda Triangle. In any 250,000 square miles (647,500 square kilometers) of ocean, disappearances are bound to happen. The Bermuda Triangle is also an area that experiences extreme weather conditions. In the case of Tutankhamun's curse, it is very probable that, when opening a tomb sealed for over 3,000 years, deadly unknown airborne bacteria could be released. This bacteria could have caused the visitors' deaths. If myths are appealing and believable, they will spread, whether or not any real evidence exists to support them.

MYSTERY, MYTH, AND PROPHECY

It is human nature to try to understand the nature of what happens around us. Until we understand unexplained events, we cannot make educated choices about how to react to them. We continue to gain more and more knowledge about the world around us, but many mysteries remain unsolved. Myths usually start as explanations for some mysterious event. Strange events occur every day, and, because it takes time to make sense of them, myths sometimes can grow to epic proportions. Some mysteries are hard to unravel because they involve the nature of human belief itself.

THE CURSE OF TUTANKHAMUN

In 1922, Howard Carter, an English archaeologist, discovered the tomb (left) of the Pharaoh Tutankhamun (1336–1327 B.C.). It is rumored that Carter destroyed an inscription in the tomb that read, "Death will slay with his wings whoever disturbs the Pharaoh's peace." A legacy of death did seem to follow the tomb's excavation. In 1923, Lord Carnarvon, who financed the excavation, died, and an archaeologist, an American financier, and a British industrialist all died after visiting the tomb. During the next seven years, twenty-two more people connected with the discovery also died, many in unusual circumstances. Carter himself, however, lived another 17 years and died at age 65.

LOST BENEATH THE WAVES

The lost continent of Atlantis (left) was said to have been the center of a highly advanced civilization. According to ancient legends, Atlantean scientists understood the human mind and were great magicians. Atlantis was said to have been destroyed by a simultaneous volcanic eruption, earthquake, and tidal wave, but some Atlanteans reportedly escaped and preserved their magical arts. No convincing geological or archaeological evidence of the existence of Atlantis has ever been found.

TITANIC DISASTER

Some disasters reportedly have been foretold. Predictions supposedly recorded before an event are later used to prove an ability to foretell the future. Before major disasters, such as the sinking of the *Titanic* (right), the event is often claimed to have been predicted, sometimes with detailed accounts of what was going to occur. One theory about these predictions is that disasters involve so many deaths they create an energy that can be felt by sensitive psychics. Although this phenomenon cannot be proven, many people who do not consider themselves psychic claim to experience premonitions of danger.

NOSTRADAMUS AND PROPHECIES

Nostradamus (1503-1566) (left) was a French doctor known for his treatment of the plague. In 1555, he published a book of obscure prophecies in the form of quatrains, or poems in four lines. His followers believe he predicted various important events in later centuries, but his prophecies are so vague that it is difficult to match them to specific incidents. The following prophecy, for example, was read as foretelling the 1945 bombing of Hiroshima and Nagasaki in Japan: "Near the harbor and in two cities will be two scourges, the like of which have never been seen. Hunger, plague within, people thrown out by the sword will cry for help from the great immortal God."

BOARD GAMES

The Ouija board has been used since the 1850s to contact spirits. It was once a triangular board supported by two wheels and a pencil. The pressure of people's hands placed on the board's surface moved the board, and the pencil wrote messages, supposedly from spirits, on a piece of paper beneath it. In 1868, American toy companies refined the idea. In their "game," participants place their hands on a planchette, or small triangular board, that moves across another larger board featuring letters of the alphabet and the words *yes* and *no* (right). The planchette moves from letter to letter to spell out a message. The "spirit" message, however, can be faked by players controlling the planchette.

RECEPTIVE MINDS

Meditation (opposite) is a technique used to clear and calm the mind. Many psychics use meditation to prepare their minds to receive telepathic thoughts or messages from the spirit world. Meditation also is used in prayer, in healing, and as a relaxation technique. Many types of yoga, for example, make use of meditation. Prolonged meditation may send a person into a trancelike state in which the entire mind is concentrated on a single thought.

MUSIC FROM THE GRAVE

Some mediums specialize in contacting the spirits of dead celebrities. Rosemary Brown (1916-2001), a London housewife, claimed she had been contacted by the spirits of eminent composers, such as Beethoven (right), who supposedly dictated musical scores to her. Rosemary's lack of musical training meant she was only able to produce fragments, but experts have said her work appears to be more than just imitation. Another medium, Stella Horrocks, produces whole novels that she claims have been dictated to her by dead authors. She goes into a trance to write, and the handwriting for each novelist is different.

EXORCISM

In the Bible, exorcisms were performed to cast out demons who had possessed a person's body (above). Some religious leaders still perform exorcisms. As in the past, these rituals are intended to rid a person or place of spirits. An exorcist commands the possessing spirit to leave and often uses the name of God to enforce his or her will. Some exorcisms require three items to perform the ritual: a Bible, a bell, and a candle. Some people believe humans cannot be possessed by spirits; what is seen as a spirit possession may actually be a form of mental illness or hallucinations.

THE POWERFUL MIND

Many psychics and mediums believe the spirit world can be reached through the unconscious mind. Some psychics believe people unknowingly, or unconsciously, leave psychic images of themselves wherever they go. Police occasionally have hired psychics to help catch criminals. Some of these psychics supposedly identify criminals by reading psychic impressions the criminals left at a crime scene. Psychics also have been known to track down missing people, both alive and dead. Many techniques, including hypnosis, reportedly are used to contact the supernatural world through the power of the unconscious mind. The sheer variety of methods is one reason why scientists have found it difficult to investigate supposed psychic abilities.

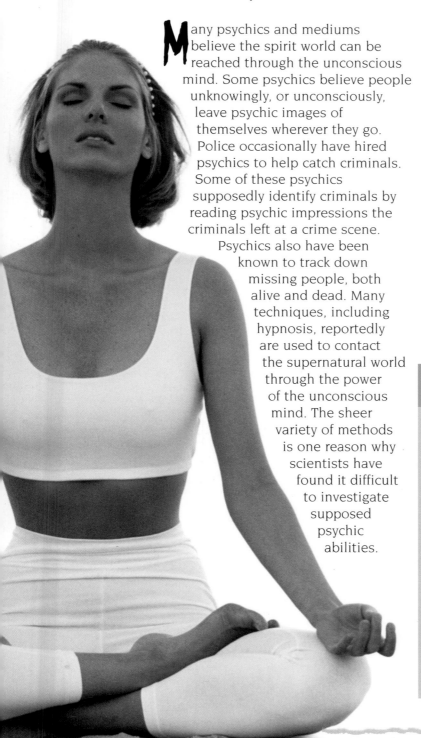

AUTOMATIC WRITING

Some people believe that when a person writes without conscious control, he or she is writing messages from spirits. One method of writing in this way involves going into a trance while staring at a candle's reflection in a mirror (above) and holding a pen or pencil. This unconscious, or "automatic," writing is usually disjointed and incomprehensible, but some people treat it as if it is full of meaning. Others have doubts; they believe the trancelike state can easily be faked.

What do YOU think

Some people believe spirits can be controlled or contacted by living people through the power of rituals. Whether they are trying to banish a spirit or asking a spirit for help, people use music, words, special items, certain mental preparations, or some combination of these to open up a link between themselves and the spirit. The purpose of the ritual may be to strengthen or weaken the spirit's hold on the ordinary, earthly world. The ritual also may be intended to affect the person who is conducting it by raising the person's own spirit to a "higher plane."

TERMS USED IN DIVINATION

astrology: using signs of the zodiac to tell the future

cartomancy: using playing cards to tell the future

catoptromancy: using mirrors to tell the future

chiromancy: reading the lines on a person's hand to see the person's future or character

geomancy: observing land forms or the patterns made by dust on a flat surface to tell the future

metascopy: using lines on a person's forehead to tell his or her future

necromancy: conjuring or contacting the spirits of the dead to tell the future

oneiromancy: using dreams to tell the future

rhabdomancy: using rods or wands for divination, especially in dowsing for water or treasure (see page 24)

CROSS MY PALM WITH SILVER

Foretelling the future in exchange for a fee is a practice that has been around in many cultures for centuries, Today, however, many people associate this practice with the Romany, or gypsy, culture. Traditionally, people with a Romany heritage were seen as having strong psychic powers. Gypsies, who used to travel widely across Europe, were seen as accomplished fortune-tellers. A crystal ball was used by some of these fortune-tellers. They claimed they could divine the future by looking into its depths.

DIVINATION

When a person practices "divination," he or she foretells the future or reveals what is hidden by supposedly mystical or supernatural means. Many of the divining methods that have been used for centuries still are used today. Divination often involves a set of symbols or marks that are said to represent emotions, events, or personal qualities. By selecting these symbols seemingly at random or by observing symbols that occur in a particular pattern, fortune-tellers make predictions about the future.

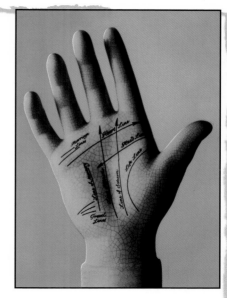

PALM READING

Palmistry, or chiromancy, is a form of divination that involves interpreting lines on the palm of a person's hand. Palmists associate certain lines on the palm (above) with certain aspects of a person's life. The aspects associated with each line have developed gradually and differ among palmists, but they generally include life, health, fortune, and fate. Breaks and bends in the various lines signify important events in a person's life.

THE ZODIAC

The Ram, the Bull, the Heavenly Twins.
Next to the Crab, the Lion shines, the Virgin and the Scales.
The Scorpion, Archer and He-Goat,
The man who carries the Watering Pot and the
Fish with the glittering tails.

This verse, called "The Hunt of the Heavenly Host," helps people remember the twelve astrological symbols that make up the zodiac (above), an astrological system used in several divining techniques. At the time of a person's birth, the position of the planets, the Sun, the Moon, and the stars that make up the signs of the zodiac are believed to permanently affect the person's nature. The signs are divided into four groups associated with four main elements: earth, fire, air, and water. Leo, for example, is a fire sign. According to the zodiac system, a person born under the sign of Leo is associated with adventure and ambition.

What do YOU think ?

Is divination really just good guesswork? Accomplished fortune-tellers can make educated guesses about the future of a client simply by looking at his or her appearance or quickly studying behavior. Predicting good fortune for someone who admits to being hardworking, for example, has a good chance of being accurate.

CASTING THE ORACLE

Looking at the stars or gazing into a crystal ball are not the only ways people can try to divine the future. Some fortune tellers toss objects or select them at random and read the patterns they make. Ancient practitioners called this method of divination "casting the oracle." Originally, the objects used were simple items easily made or found in nature, such as sticks. Over the years, more and more rituals have developed around casting, and the cards, stones, and sticks used have become more elaborate and decorative.

FORTUNE-TELLING WITH TEA LEAVES

Reading tea leaves is a simple form of divination. After a person drinks all the tea in his or her cup, a diviner turns the cup counterclockwise three times. The diviner then "reads" the patterns the leaves form (above) to predict coming events. The Romany, or gypsies, have a symbolic language they use to interpret the patterns. Leaves in the shape of a padlock, for example, mean a door to success is about to open.

RUNE STONES

Casting rune stones is an ancient Scandinavian form of divination. The word *runa* is an Anglo-Saxon term meaning "mystery." Rune Masters were magicians who supposedly used the power of a hidden language written on stones in runes (right), or characters, to affect the weather, the harvest, healing, war, and love. The traditional Germanic set of rune stones uses an alphabet of three sets of eight runes. Later stone sets include a blank stone to represent the unknowable. To "read" the stones, a diviner draws them unseen from a pouch and lays them down in a specific pattern. The pattern helps the diviner determine their meaning in relation to a given question.

DOWSING FOR WATER

Dowsing (left) is using a rod or wand to find something hidden or buried in the ground, such as water, treasures, or lost objects. Some dowsers reportedly can find electrical cables, mineral deposits, or oil. Traditionally, a water dowser holds a forked stick out over the ground as he or she walks. If water is under the ground, the stick, or dowsing rod, twitches. It has been suggested that dowsers are simply people who are particularly sensitive to Earth's magnetic field. Some dowsers, however, have found water and other items by holding a pendulum over a map.

THE MAGICIAN.

ⲃ The Magician ☿

TAROT

Tarot cards are a special set of cards used for divination. Instead of using the four playing card suits of hearts, spades, diamonds, and clubs, Tarot cards use the suits of cups, swords, wands, and disks. The deck also contains the Major Arcana—twenty-two cards that are not part of any suit. Each card has a different symbolic association. Different Tarot decks, however, offer different designs and different symbolic associations for each card. The Magician (left and above), for example, could appear physically different and could mean willpower or skill, depending on the Tarot deck used. During a Tarot reading, a reader lays cards face down in certain patterns to focus on different aspects of a person's life. The cards are then turned over one by one and interpreted.

THE I CHING

One of the oldest books of oracles in the world, the Chinese I Ching or Book of Changes has lasted in its present form for at least three thousand years. Diviners do not use the I Ching to predict specific events. Instead, the book shows possible outcomes of certain actions. It is composed of sixty-four hexagrams in different combinations of six broken or unbroken lines. A diviner performs random activities, such as drawing straws from a bundle (opposite) or tossing coins, to produce a hexagram and then uses the I Ching to determine the meaning of the hexagram.

What do YOU think

Divination methods can be grouped into two categories. Some divination methods involve interpreting random events—such as the pattern in which tea leaves are left in a cup. Other methods involve studying a person's physical qualities—such as lines in the palm of a hand. The difference between these two categories is important. It may be easier to believe that a person's character might express itself through the lines on his or her palm than to believe a person's mere presence can affect the pattern of tea leaves in a cup. The methods of divination that involve random events may also give the diviner time to judge a person's character, so the diviner can make up an appropriate prediction for the person's future.

DREAMS AND VISIONS

Scientists did not make a concerted effort to study the human mind or psyche until the twentieth century. Psychology, the study of the human mind and behavior, and neuroscience, the study of the brain, are therefore still young sciences. Scientists are still investigating the processes of the unconscious mind. One important early psychologist, Sigmund Freud (1856-1939), suggested dreams play a major role in how the unconscious mind works. Carl Jung (1875-1961) later proposed that we all share one collective, or group, unconscious in which certain images recur. Each image, he noted, has its own symbolism. Parapsychology, the study of psychic phenomena, draws on psychology and neuroscience. Scientists still have much to learn in all of these fields.

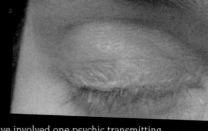

KUBLA KHAN'S PLEASURE DOME

In 1797, the poet Samuel Taylor Coleridge (1772-1834) (above) reportedly composed three hundred lines of poetry in a dream while sleeping. When he woke, he remembered the poem and began to write it down. After a visitor interrupted him, however, he was unable to recall the rest of the poem. He published *Kubla Khan*, the remembered portion of the poem, in 1816. Many other writers, musicians, and artists have also reported gaining inspiration from their dreams. Parapsychologists suggest we all have a "sixth" sense, a sense of paranormal sensory information (PSI). This sense is supposedly weak but functions best when we have no distractions, such as when we sleep.

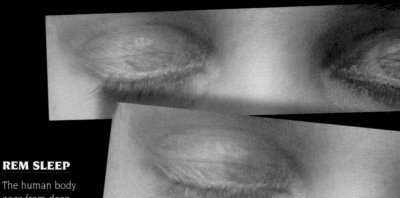

REM SLEEP

The human body goes from deep to light sleep in five stages. During the rapid eye movement (REM) stage of deep sleep (right), the mind is active and a person dreams. People dream every time they sleep, even if they do not always remember their dreams. A technique known as lucid dreaming trains the sleeping mind to control the progress of dreams.

SLEEP RESEARCH

Studies conducted on sleeping people have indicated people are better able to receive psychic messages while they are in the rapid eye movement (REM) stage of sleep. Paranormal experiments have involved one psychic transmitting images to another, sleeping psychic at different stages of the sleep cycle. The sleeping psychic was awakened after each stage of sleep and could recall the images most successfully after the REM stage.

ANALYSIS OF DREAMS

People have many theories and beliefs about dreams. Some ancient peoples believed they were messages from the gods. Sigmund Freud, one of the first scientists who studied dreaming, thought dreams were the wishes of the unconscious mind. More recently, Carl Jung (right) wrote that in dreams people harness their creativity and come to terms with their fears. Modern sleep research tends to indicate that dreams are the result of neurons firing in the brain during the process of storing memories. Dreams are also closely linked with the study of psychic phenomena.

OUT-OF-BODY EXPERIENCES

Some people have reportedly had out-of-body experiences. In these experiences, people are usually near death and often report seeing a bright light or feeling as if the spirit, or soul, is being pulled away from the body. They often report having watched their own unconscious human body being revived, while they exist in an "astral" body. This astral body is claimed to be identical to the physical body but is transparent and shining. Ancient writings describe this phenomenon as a supernatural power that can be gained through magic or meditation. Skeptics suggest people having these experiences were hallucinating or delusional at the time.

What do YOU think ?

Many people believe dreams and so-called psychic visions are caused by the mind behaving oddly when it is on the edge of consciousness. Surrealist artists such as Salvador Dali (1904-1989) would put themselves into a semi-conscious state on purpose. They believed that in this state they were in touch with a higher "level" of reality. They painted the images they saw and believed these images spoke directly to the unconscious mind. Most people probably think they also dream complex, strange, and interesting dreams that would make wonderful paintings, books, or films—if only they were remembered and could be reproduced on paper!

EXPERIMENTS OF THE MIND

Parapsychology is the study of extraordinary mental—or so-called psychic—phenomena that are reportedly experienced by humans yet seem to have no physical cause. Parapsychology research includes investigating extrasensory perception (ESP), psychokinesis (PK), and out-of-body experiences. ESP is the ability to receive paranormal sensory information (PSI) not available to the five senses, while PK (also known as telekinesis) is the ability to change the state of physical objects or move them by mental activity alone. The study of parapsychology assumes that the potential of the human mind has been underestimated. Many scientists, however, do not treat parapsychology as a "real" science because it has become falsely associated with other, unrelated paranormal events, such as alien abductions.

TELEPATHY

Paranormal research reportedly has recorded many instances of telepathy. Telepathy is the communication of thoughts without speaking or signing (above). People who are closely related, especially twins, supposedly tend to have a better chance of experiencing a telepathic connection. Paranormal researchers have performed experiments in which people communicate telepathically over long distances, and they report impressive results. For many people, however, these experiments have yet to prove beyond a doubt that telepathic communication exists.

PHOTOGRAPHING AURAS

Many mediums have claimed they can see an aura, a visible field of energy, coming from the human body. In 1939, Semyon Kirlian, a Russian engineer, invented a medical device that supposedly could photograph electrical and other energies given off by the human body. He photographed these "auras" using an electric coil, an aluminum plate, and photosensitive film covered by glass. His pictures (opposite) showed people surrounded by a colored light.

JOSEPH RHINE

In 1927, Dr. Joseph Rhine and his wife Louisa (below) started the first investigations into ESP at Duke University in North Carolina. These investigations marked the beginning of the science of parapsychology. Rhine invented the term ESP and spent fifty years researching the phenomenon. His work was first published in 1934. Many scientists, however, immediately found fault with his laboratory techniques and analysis of statistics. Although Rhine defended his work, many still thought his experiments were not valid.

MILITARY APPLICATIONS OF PSI

Throughout history, people have been trying to find ways for psychic phenomena to serve as a source of protection. During the Cold War, the U.S. and Soviet governments reportedly performed studies on paranormal sensory information (PSI) to see how it could be used by their militaries. For some years, a secret U.S. defense project at the Pentagon (above), known as Operation Stargate, was said to be training psychics. The psychics supposedly were being trained to use their abilities to see into enemy bases or to cause mental confusion in military leaders.

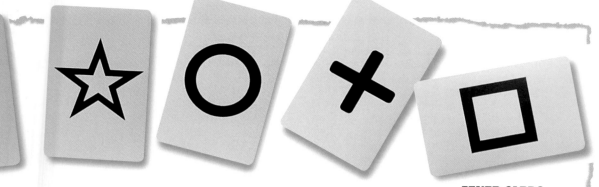

Zener cards (above) were used in some of the earliest experiments on psychic abilities. Zener cards are a deck of twenty-five cards divided into five sets of five symbols. To perform the experiment, the scientist shuffles the cards. The test subject then attempts to use PSI to guess the order of the cards. To test telepathy, one person looks at a card and tries to telepathically communicate the symbol on the card to someone across the room. Dr. Rhine reportedly had a high success rate with his experiments. Some subjects were even able to predict what order the cards would be shuffled into before they were shuffled.

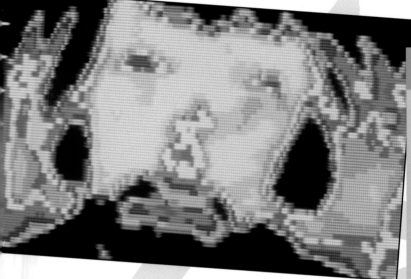

What do YOU think ?

Statistically, everyone has a one in five chance of correctly guessing which Zener symbol has been drawn from a deck. If a person guesses correctly many more times than one in five, then that person may have extrasensory perception, or ESP. Parapsychology experiments, however, rarely have been taken seriously because many scientists doubt the experiments actually prove the existence of psychic abilities. It is difficult to design an experiment that makes it impossible for anyone to accuse the researcher of faking the results. There is always a possibility that if a researcher is convinced a phenomenon exists, the researcher will see what he or she wants to see in the results.

MESMERIZING MINDS

Franz Mesmer (1734-1815), an Austrian doctor, believed the human body has magnetic properties that can be used to cure illness. Mesmer performed public "healings" that involved using cords to connect people to a tub of water filled with iron filings (left). He had some success, but scientists at the time remained unconvinced, and he was declared an impostor. Although Mesmer's work was largely discredited, it paved the way for the study of hypnosis and the unconscious mind.

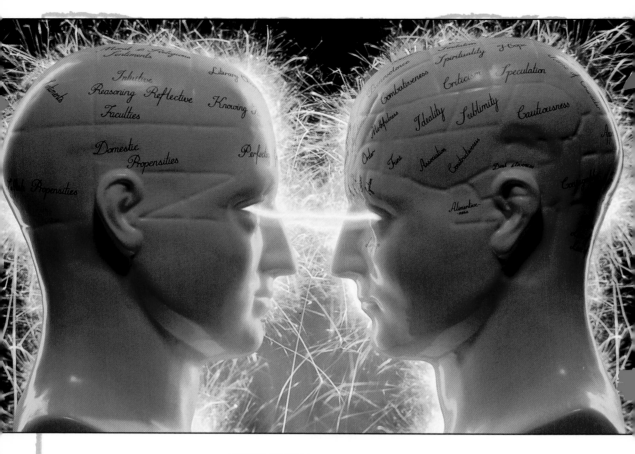

BRAIN WAVES

Recently, paranormal researchers have been trying to understand what exactly happens in the brain during telepathic communication or other psychic activity. During a psychic episode, researchers have recorded the patterns of a test subject's brain waves, or electrical pulses in the brain (above). Some studies reportedly show that some brain waves do indeed change during psychic activity.

SOVIET STUDIES

The Soviet Union was one of the first countries to do official scientific research into psychic phenomena. In 1926, Soviet scientists investigated what physical conditions were needed to allow a person's mind to send out energy. In the 1960s and 1970s, they did many studies of Nina Kulagina (left), a Russian housewife. They reportedly discovered that under controlled laboratory conditions, Kulagina could move objects, create burn marks on them, and increase their magnetic properties—all without ever touching the objects.

ESP AND PK

The two most widely researched areas of psychic phenomena are extrasensory perception (ESP) and psychokinesis (PK), or telekinesis. ESP includes telepathy, or the communication of thoughts without signing or speaking, and precognition, or the prediction of future events. PK, on the other hand, involves the change in state or the movement of objects solely through the power of the mind. Reports of poltergeists, or invisible ghosts who move objects or make noise, may actually be instances of PK. Some people believe a teenager whose body is undergoing enormous chemical and physical changes could cause PK without knowing it. Somehow, the chemical activity in his or her body affects the environment.

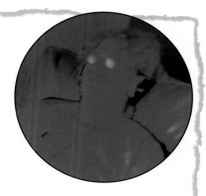

RANDOM NUMBERS, DEFINITE RESULTS

Parapsychologists have performed many experiments to measure whether humans can influence the outcome of a random event. In the past, experiments included asking test subjects to try and influence what numbers would come up when dice were rolled. Now scientists can use random number generator (RNG) machines to perform experiments that are reportedly harder to fake. An RNG machine produces a stream of numbers selected at random. Unlike the roll of dice, a test subject cannot affect the machine's stream by any physical means. Researchers have performed experiments to see if humans can influence what numbers the machine will produce. The experiments reportedly show that most humans *can* influence which numbers will come up randomly. The success rate reportedly is higher when there is a full moon; at that time, the electromagnetic energy in the brain may be affected by Earth's magnetic field.

GANZFELD EXPERIMENTS

In a *ganzfeld*, or total field, experiment, test subjects are first placed in an environment that is free of almost all sensory information, including sights, sounds, and smells (above). When the subjects reach a relaxed and receptive state, the experiment begins. One subject, a "sender," attempts to telepathically communicate a random image to another subject, the "receiver." The receiver reports aloud all his or her thoughts, images, feelings, and impulses, so scientists can determine if the telepathy was a success. The ganzfeld experiment reportedly has achieved a high success rate. More subjects successfully sent and received images than would have been possible by pure chance alone.

PSYCHOKINESIS

In the 1920s, Baron Albert von Schrenk-Notzing, an investigator of the paranormal, worked with psychics Stanislava Tomczyk (right) and Willy Schneider to convince scientific observers and members of the English Society for Psychical Research that it was possible to levitate objects without any physical means. Many people who witnessed the psychics' works believed in their abilities.

PLACES OF POWER

Despite all of the research into reported psychic phenomena, many of these events remain a mystery. Over the centuries, their mystery has inspired many attempts to harness the powers of the unknown. Today, supposed places of intense psychic power are scattered across the world. Some are natural sites that are considered sacred. Others were built as centers for religious practices or magic rituals. Many of these ancient places continue to symbolize the psychic forces we do not yet understand.

POWER LINES

Ley lines supposedly are channels of power that run across Earth's surface. They often connect ancient religious sites or centers of special energy. Some people suggest ley lines are natural features of Earth, while others believe ancient civilizations created the lines. Some people believe dowsers can harness the power in these lines to help them find water or metals. Ley lines are said to be detected by variations in radio waves. In England, ley lines are believed to cross Glastonbury Tor (above), a place of great religious significance.

THE PYRAMIDS

The pyramids at Giza in Egypt are some of the oldest surviving human-made structures in the world. Egyptian pharoahs had the pyramids constructed, possibly as tombs for their mummified bodies and the possessions they believed they would take into the afterlife. From the dimensions of one of these pyramids, the Great Pyramid (right), modern mathematicians have discovered that ancient Egyptians knew the value of *pi*, a mathematical value involved in determining the circumference of a circle. They also knew the number of days Earth takes to circle the Sun and, possibly, the dates of important events in the future. Recently, it has been suggested that the pyramids' positions match the layout of the stars in the Orion constellation.

SACRED SITES OF THE ANCESTORS

Ayers Rock (left), or Uluru, in the Northern Territory of Australia is the largest single rock formation in the world. The place has a strong spiritual significance for many Aboriginal people. The Aborigines keep many of their stories about Uluru secret, and many of their ancestral sites can be found in the area. Out of respect for Aboriginal beliefs, the Australian government has restricted tourist access to these sites.

STANDING STONES

Stonehenge (right) in Great Britain was built around 1200 B.C. Today, people still do not know why it was built. It may have been used as an observatory for the stars, a religious center, or a burial ground. In 1977, the Dragon Project was established to study electrical and magnetic forces around Stonehenge and similar monuments. Other standing stone monuments include Carnac in Brittany, Msoura in Morocco, and the monuments at Lake Turkana in Kenya.

What do YOU think ?

Many people feel a sense of awe and mystery when visiting one of the places that are centers of reported psychic power. Even people who might not believe these places are centers of power often are amazed. The vision, dedication, effort, and genius that went into the construction of sites such as Stonehenge or the Pyramids can be impressive.

DID YOU KNOW?

During a war in Poland in 1430, a group of Hussite soldiers slashed a painting of the Madonna, the mother of Jesus Christ. Despite repeated attempts to repair the painting, the slashes reportedly have always reappeared.

During an experiment in psychokinesis (PK), a blank piece of paper was left in a typewriter. The typewriter was then guarded against all possibilities of anyone using it. Some time later, however, the paper was examined and the following unsigned verse was found.

A *clever man*, W.E. *Cox*
Made a really remarkable box
In it, we, with PK
In the usual way
W*rote, spite of bands, seals*
and locks.

New Zealand's rugby team, the All Blacks, perform a ceremonial ritual called the *haka taparahi* before all of their matches. In the tradition of the Maori people, the energetic chant and dance is intended to bring the team good fortune in the match.

THE MAGICIAN.

Ouija is a combination of the French word *oui* and the German word *ja*, both of which mean "yes."

In the Bible, the prophet Elisha is said to have sent his spirit into the tent of a Syrian king to frustrate his plans to destroy the Israelites.

Padre Pio, a well-known twentieth-century Italian priest, reportedly could perform bilocation, or be in two places at the same time. One night, Padre Pio apparently knocked on the door of the Archbishop of Montevideo in Uruguay. Pio informed the Archbishop that one of his priests was dying. Sometime later, the Archbishop met Pio again. Pio confirmed that he had been in Uruguay that night, although he had never physically left Italy.

The Australian Skeptics group is offering 80,000 Australian dollars to anyone who can prove the existence of ESP, telepathy, or telekinesis. The prize has been offered since 1980 and is still waiting to be won.

FOR FURTHER INFORMATION

WEB SITES

Zener Card Online ESP Test **moebius.psy.ed.ac.uk/~paul/zener.html**

Harry Houdini Online Exhibit by the Outagamie County Historical Society **www.akahoudini.org/htdocs/index.php**

Ayers Rock, or Ulurul **www.walkabout.com.au/locations/NTUluru.shtml**

The Skeptic's Dictionary of the Supernatural and Paranormal **www.skepdic.com/**

BOOKS

Bailey, Gerald. *Prophecies: Can You See into the Future?* Elements of the Extraordinary series (Element Books)

Gorman, Jacqueline Laks. *ESP.* X Science series (Gareth Stevens)

Mason, Paul. *Investigating the Supernatural.* Forensic Files series (Heinemann)

Weist-Meyer, Mariam. *Mysteries of the Mind.* Great Unsolved Mysteries (Steck-Vaughn)

anti-clerical—against the Christian clergy, such as pastors or priests

astrological—relating to the study of the supposed effects the positions of stars, planets, and other heavenly bodies have on human affairs

clairvoyants—people who can perceive beyond the normal range of human senses

discredit—destroy or injure the credibility of or confidence in the reliability of a person, belief or practice

fraud—deceit or tricks done for profit; an imposter, or someone who is not who she or he pretends to be

hallucination—an image or a sound a person sees or hears but that does not really exist outside the mind

hemophilia—a genetic disorder that causes a person to bleed excessively from minor injuries because an abnormality in the blood prevents the blood from clotting, or forming scabs.

hypnosis—a trancelike state characterized by a readiness to respond to suggestions. This state resembles sleep and is artificially induced in one person by another person

hysteria—a state of intense fear, anxiety, or excitement

incomprehensible—not able to be understood

infuse—pour into or cause to penetrate

interpreting—explaining the meaning of something

levitating—rising or floating in the air, apparently without being affected by gravity

mediums—people through whom spirits of the dead supposedly contact the living

oracle—priest or priestess who can reportedly ask questions of and receive answers from a god or goddess; an answer or pronouncement that is treated as unquestionably wise and valid

paranormal—unable to be explained by scientific reasons

phenomenon (*pl.* phenomena)—an act or an object perceived by the senses; a rare event

premonitions—forewarnings; feelings of anxiety over a coming event

psychic—(adj.) outside the area of natural or scientific knowledge, often nonphysical or spiritual in force; (n.) a person who can sense supernatural or nonphysical forces

refute—prove that something is false or in error

regurgitate—vomit or spit up

relic—an object of interest because of its age or association with past events

supernatural—not being of the visible, earthly world; ghostly

superstitions—beliefs or practices not based on logic but rather resulting from fear of the unknown, misunderstanding the causes for events, or belief in magic

susceptible—able to be easily influenced or affected emotionally; open to or not resistant to a certain influence

valid—well-founded, justifiable, or having the weight of authority